confessi
a fearless heart

carol chaves wilber

dedication:

to my loving husband, who came into my life and loved me like it was the easiest thing he's ever done, and when it wasn't, he still chose to stay. I couldn't thank God enough for you, Caleb ♡

re were days
wn myself thinking about you
 miss you so much
 know what to do with myself
 I'd forget to breath for a second
ght of losing you again would torment

r would hunt me
rkest alleys inside my mind
run
as backed up in a corner
out any hope left to grip onto
 it in the eyes
race it with a tight hug
it how it feels
ll me
els
nted

prologue:

"it either turns into love,
or into a poem"

that was my motto when I started my journey
looking for love…

well,

it turned into so many poems that now I have a
whole book for you ;)

stop being scared every time
something good happens in your life,
stop overthinking every time
you meet someone you like,
stop pushing people away every time
you start caring about them a little too much,
not everybody is going to hurt you,
not everyone is going to leave you,
you are going to be happy
good things are going to happen to you
there are real I love you's
there are great friends waiting to meet you
allow yourself to believe that
allow yourself to be who you were created to be
live the life God has blessed you with
there are going to be better days and of course,
the sun will rise again tomorrow and you can
try again…

"a letter from me now to myself then"

I'll practice my patienc
I'll sit here and watch
while you play
and shuffle through he
wasting all your good
on players who's mind
are fixed on the wrong

and th
I'd dro
I woul
I didn'
so mu
the tho
me
that fea
in the
and I'd
until I
and wit
I'd stare
and emi
and ask
please
how it f
to be w

God's love
set me free
from things
I didn't even know I was chained to

you made me feel so safe
that vulnerability came easily
and so I opened up to you
I gave you access to a deeper part of me
a part of me that you didn't deserve

"I should've guarded my heart"

the more you hurt me,
the more you push me away,

the more I learn to depend on myself
the more I learn to be there for myself

the less you love me
the more you teach me
to love myself

but what am I supposed to do
when both my goal and obstacle are the same:
you

for so long
I held on
I held on to whatever you left me with
for so long
I refused to believe
that you never felt what I did
that you never **loved** how I did

but at the end of the day
if you really had felt what I did
you wouldn't have let go
at least not like that
not that easy

"mysterious girl"

it's what he called me
he said he wanted to get to know me more
so I let him,
I let him in
and I watched his eyes open as wide as the
ocean
when he looked around
pacing slowly inside the forest of my brain…

…it wasn't long till he couldn't take it anymore
"I feel trapped, I can't breath" he would say
as the tall trees closed up above him
"everything feels like it's falling down on me"
his words would've cut deep if I hadn't heard
them before
but he was just another guy
who failed to realize that he was walking
through a place
I had built to get away from the world…

…when **I felt trapped and couldn't breath,**
when everything felt like it was falling down on
me

the forest was my refugee
and what he called chaos was where I found my
peace

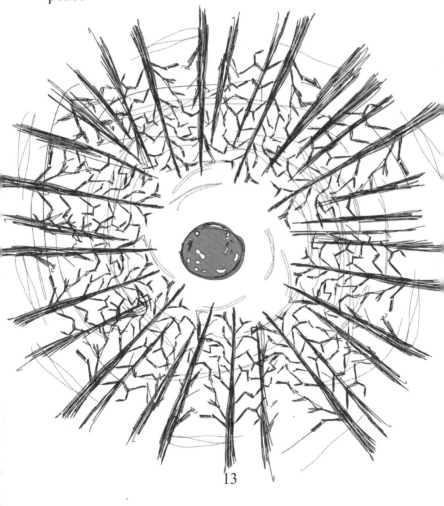

our hands were locked together
as we ran like little kids
side by side
while laughing at ourselves
and when we reached the edge
we looked into each other eyes
we were talking
without saying a word
and I really thought
we were on the same page
when I jumped
without thinking twice
but I felt my heart sink
heavier than your consciousness
when my eyes
finally met yours again
but this time
you were looking from a distance
down at me
from up there

I'm stuck in this deep and dark hole
it's so cold and lonely
but I get up every morning
and look up at the light above
it seems so far away

every now and then you stop by
and you look at me from up there
you watch me struggle to get out
but you never offer help

I think now
you like seeing me stuck and
helpless
because you know it's the only way
to keep me around
you realize if you set me free
I would leave and never look
back

*"the danger of falling for someone
who doesn't love you but doesn't want to
lose you"*

and when they walked in there
looking for art full of colors

I watched them pass by me through the hallways
with a quick glance before moving forward

the weight of the truth hit me so hard
my frame almost fell to the floor
no one wants a gray painting
but at that point
it was all I had to offer

"what trying to date after you was like"

I painted my canvas blue
because it was your favorite color
waiting on the wall for you to pass by

then I watched you in the hallway
look at me and
keep walking…

because what you were looking for
wasn't art

you held my hand
looked me in the eyes
and told me to trust you
and I did
before I realized I was following your footsteps
I didn't even know where we were headed
it didn't matter
my eyes were focused on yours
and I saw flames in them
it was freeing…
till it wasn't

I finally looked around me
and realized the flames in your eyes
were just a reflection of the fire you set me on
I was burning

he said *I love you*
and even though she said it back
he could see it in her eyes
she didn't understand what that meant
and that was the day
he decided he would do everything in his power
to show her

the truth is,
regardless of everything we have been through
and everything we HAVEN'T
deep down inside my heart
I still want it to be you
so bad
with every bone in my body
with every ounce of hope left in my soul

and I've even considered
that maybe it's not you
that maybe there's someone out there
that will know how to love me the way you didn't
but no matter how far I let my mind wonder
I always find myself
coming back to **you**

"you never really knew me"

you said
and maybe you were right
but…
heaven knows I really tried to

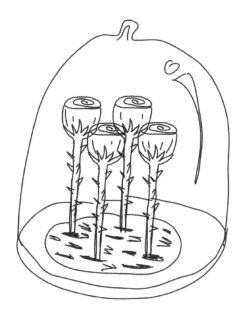

I want to be loved
I crave it
so badly
and I hope with everything in me
it can come from you
because there's no one else in this world
id want that kind of love from...

it still hurts…

I keep telling myself
that you just don't know how to love me

but maybe,
maybe you do
because I know you're capable of it
I know it because I've seen it
I've felt it
or at least   b i t s   of it
I've gotten the *taste* of it at times
a love so sweet and pure

before you ripped it away so cruelly
and left me there with the cold heartbreaking truth:

it's not that you don't *know* how to love me
you simply **choose** not to…

I was so busy
this whole time
trying to be there for you
trying to love you
that I forgot to love myself
and now I know
I needed it too

the thing is
I don't mind being alone
in fact, I actually enjoy it

it just gets hard
when it's not a **choice**

*"I used to enjoy saturdays alone
before you came around"*

"a poem about letting go"

and one night
one night I just got tired
I got tired of waiting
tired of trying to make sense
of the mess you left me with
I got tired of trying
trying to understand
why you did what you did
and mainly
why you didn't do what you should've

"can you see me?"

I watched you
go from date to date
girl to girl
looking for the same thing
and failing to find it

and for a while
I looked at the one in the mirror and thought
"what is wrong? what is missing?"

only to realize
the problem wasn't me
you were distracting yourself
drowning in your pride and ego
and refusing to look at what was
right in front of you
this whole time

I gave you what you needed
but you didn't want it from me

you didn't give me what I needed
but I wanted it from you

"the irony of us"

I loved you
I loved you in all the ways I knew how to
and in the ways I didn't…

I learned
just for you

"what falling for you felt
like…"

I was a fish
taken from a small aquarium
and released it into the ocean
where the waters seem endless
and the waves are promising
where the eye opening truth flows
around freely
bringing the hope that there's more out there

eventually they bring me back *"home"*
back to that little aquarium on someones nightstand
where nothing ever seems to change
and even though everything around me was the same
I wasn't

your love was my ocean
I only got a taste of it before I had to leave
now I go from water to water
without the desire to swim again
Im not sure its possible
to know your love and not swim in your ocean

31

"gaslight"

don't make me feel bad
don't try to change my mind
you've made your choices
and now it's time for me to make mine

you took my love
and turned it into fuel
fuel for your ego
so you could use it to chase
in other girls
what you had already found in me

and I was so afraid to let go
afraid to let you go
thinking I'd never find anyone like you
thinking I'd never find any love like this
when in reality

shouldn't **you** be the one…
…scared?
my love for you was **real**
and it was there
while your love for me was just
a *figment of my imagination*
a projection of everything my heart has ever
wanted
and you were who I chose to believe in

I'd be walking away of *what could've been*
while you'd be walking away from **what it was**

and it was…
something beautiful

I've always wondered why they call it
falling in love
not rising in love
but now…
now I get it
***thank you* for showing me**

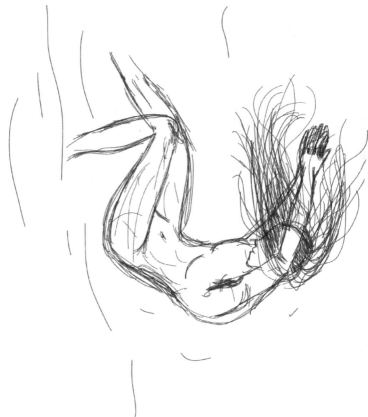

"I wanna feel colors"

I wanna feel orange
like the warmth of a sunset on a summer
afternoon
I wanna feel green
like the pain in your stomach when you're
laughing so hard you can feel your youth
through your veins
I wanna feel yellow
like the smile in your eyes after seeing a loved
one you've been missing for a while
I wanna feel purple
like the winter sky after a long rainy day
painting a beautiful sunset in the clouds
I wanna feel pink
like the feeling you get when you see their
name pop up on your phone after they've been
consuming your thought all day long
and most of all
I wanna feel red
like-
like…
like how you were supposed to show me…

my fear of ending up alone kept me there
my fear of never finding someone paralyzed me

until I realized that

begging someone to love you
is far worst
than loneliness itself

maybe I read the signs wrong
maybe I hoped for too much
or maybe this was a beautiful love story
before you messed it all up

but the truth is
it doesn't matter anymore
because there's nothing else I can do
I'm exhausted of pouring my love out in vein
my knees are bruised from being on this floor
and my hands are bleeding
picking up the pieces
and trying to put them back together

I fell for you
I fell hard
but what no one showed me was
how to pull the breaks
and that's all I could think of
when the butterflies in my stomach
started turning into moths
when I finally stopped covering my eyes
and looked down
and saw where I was about to land
if I kept falling

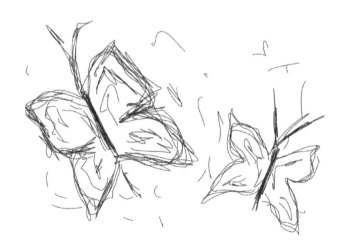

even though you didn't tell me with your words
you still showed me with your actions
that I wasn't enough for you

and **it hurt**
it hurt like that place

until I realized I wasn't the problem
you were chasing something I couldn't offer you
because all I had
was love
and what you wanted
clearly wasn't as **deep** as that

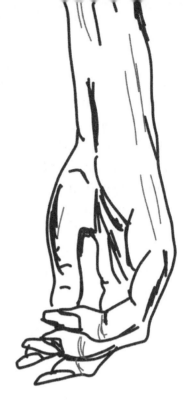

I can't hold on to you anymore
I know what we are
and I know what we are not
and I'm exhausted trying to hold on
to what we could've been

I was laying on the cold hard concrete
while the wind of the storm blew away
all my hopes and dreams
for the love story I've always wanted
and as the drops of rain pierced my skin
cutting sharp like a knife
I bled out all the love you took for granted
and wondered why I felt so cold
but I still stayed
because it made me *feel*
something

I was so focused
trying to be your gold
only to realize
you were just looking something shiny
to reflect your light

you don't know this but
you made me feel things I've never felt before

I didn't know I could feel a color
till you broke me so beautifully
that I felt blue
calm and serene
the pain was so intense that I just felt numb

it didn't surprise me
because it was expected coming from you
it didn't make me angry
because I didn't have it in me to fight anymore

I still remember the day you left
it was a cold January morning
the sun was barely out yet
and the sky was filled with grey clouds
I was outside trying to grasp some air
and suddenly it started to pour
the rain was serene yet powerful
tears slowly started rolling down my cheeks
I looked up at the sky and whispered

"me and you both…"

"blue was all you ever gave me"

and with that color
I tried to make something beautiful
so I painted myself a picture
I painted a blue sky with blue clouds
a blue ocean with blue waves
a blue sun with blue birds
I painted a love story
where I found an odd amount of comfort in
a comfort my heart had been craving for a long time

I started living in that painting
I called it **home**
util I realized I had to leave
because I was slowly drowning
in all that beautiful but melancholic

b

l

u

e

it took a while
but one day
it finally hit me…

that the only beauty in it
was what I did with what I had been given
and I finally left
when allowed myself to imagine
what I could paint
with all the colors
someone else could give me

today at 5:48pm
as I walk out of the library
I realize that around this time
I should be running to my car in excitement
because you'd be waiting for me outside
and I'd jump into your arms
and let the warmth of your presence embrace
me

but I continue walking,
because I know this time you won't be waiting
for me
and I-

I almost start to cry
right in front of the four girls sitting by the
stairs studying for their finals
and I must confess that they weren't the reason
why I didn't
my brain got ahold of my heart first
and before the tears could start rolling down
it told them that they couldn't bring you back

"I miss you so bad it hurts"

I had to roll down my windows
so that my heart could breath
through all the smoke of confusion
you were filling my lungs with
it was suffocating
and I needed to BREATH

I've taken cold showers in the early winter
mornings
I've spent late nights alone by the window
watching the snow fall
I've walked long roads while the thick
December winds burned through my skin
but nothing,
nothing,
has ever been as cold as
the look in your eyes that night
when you said
"we need to talk"

every time I gave you power over my emotions
I was sharpening your knife
and I didn't realize what are horrible mistake it was
till you cut me **so deep**
that I found myself
looking for help to stitch my heart back together

you and I
us
forever trapped in the past
now we only exist
in my memories

I stayed
longer than I should have
I stayed because I was scared
I was afraid to lose all the love you had to offer
only to realize I was waiting in vain
because even though you did have all the love
I've been thirsting to find
you'd never give it to me

I was scared to lose something I've never had...

I stood there
in front of your door
day after day
night after night
through rainbows
and through storms
breaking my pride
wasting my mind
pouring my heart
just trying to figure out a way to open it
so that I could reach you
on the other side

but as tight as I held the handle
you held the key in your pocket

and when they ask me about you
I'll tell them it wasn't love
but deep down inside I know
it was the closest to it I've ever been

I knew it was over for me
when I looked at the moon
and it made me think of you...

was it over?
or was that just the beginning?

the thought of me and you
ending up together
is so unfamiliar
that it scares me
but the thought of the alternative
is something…
I'm terrified to find out what it feels like

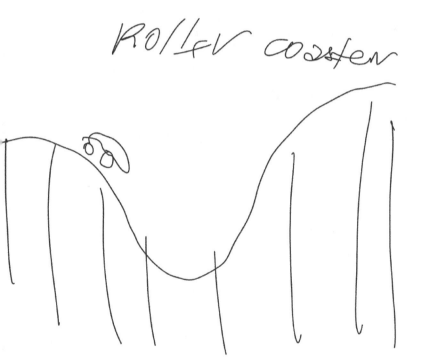

and I used to think I'd be hard to love
because the longer I stayed with you
the more I started seeing myself
the way you saw me

but now I finally see myself
as I am
through the eyes of someone who loves me

and I'm never settling for any other
version of myself
than the one
I was created to be

I wish you would've held my hand
as tight as you held on
to all the empty promises of this world

they said I was just looking for love
and ~~if~~ since you weren't able to give it to me
they told me I should *just* move on
they said eventually I'd just find it in someone else
but it wasn't till I was wrapped around his arms
and he looked into my eyes and told me he loved me
that it hit me
and I know he could read it all over my face
it didn't matter how much of it I got
it'd never be enough unless it was coming from you

I peeled my heart for you
little by little
till every inch of it was raw
open,
exposed,
fragile
and when I flinched at your aggressive touch
you called me *sensitive*

have you ever stopped to think that
maybe
just maybe
what you're really afraid of is real love?
maybe
deep dow inside you know
it's really all you want
and maybe
you believe that once you have access to it
you won't want to know a life without it
and you believe that
once its been given to you
it can be taken   a w a y

I remember when you said those words to hurt me
I could see by the look on your face
the confusion
on why nothing you said seemed to get to me
like it couldn't reach me
but what you hadn't realized was
you had taught me a while ago
not to count your words for truth

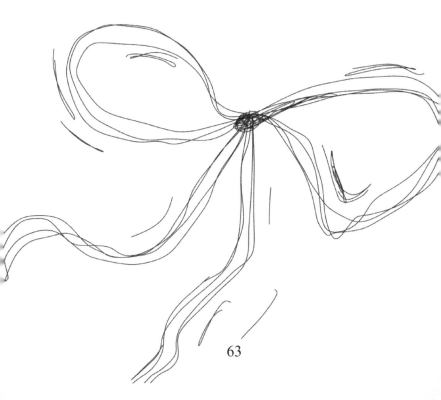

and to think that
all along
I was so scared to lose you
only to realize you were never
mine
to begin with

what a blessing it is to have memories
something to remember great times
something that never changes
even when people do…

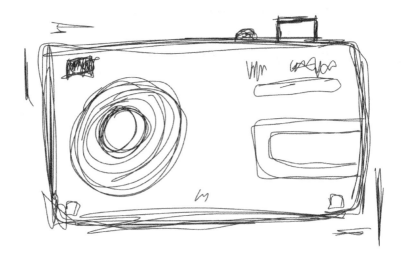

it was a cold summer night
I was on the back of your motorcycle
we were flying through the highway
my heart beat faster than the wind
my arms gripped tight around your body
holding on for my life
you felt fear through my touch
and that was when you said

"you can let your heart rest,
I won't let you get hurt…"

I know you meant that in a literal way
but you have no idea
how much I was dying to hear those words…

it wasn't until
I had placed all my cards on the table
that you picked them up and took a good look at it
just before you put them back down and
walked away
taking with you every hope I had left
that maybe if I showed a different card
you would change your mind
and **stay**

but here's the thing about love
I never learned how to take it in doses
it was always all or nothing
and I was so tired of choosing nothing
feeling nothing
that when I got a taste of your love
I decided to choose all
and just like that
I let it consume me
I did it for so long I ended up forgetting
forgetting why I was so afraid of it
but you made sure
to remind me

and when you said the love I was looking for
didn't exist
that it wasn't possible
between two humans
I knew it wasn't true
because,
I loved you that way…

all I want
is a healthy relationship
I'm done romanticizing toxic
feeding my pain with everything tossed my way
calling it love
fantasizing about what it could be
instead of looking at it for **what is is**
and mainly

what it isn't.

suddenly
our song comes on
my feet pull me up
and before I realize it
I'm on a stage
the spotlight is shining on me
my body slowly starts moving
gracefully shifting through each melody being
played
my heart knows this dance
it's all so familiar
I've heard this before
I've danced this before
only last time you were here to dance with me

"what trying to fall in love again feels like"

71

and I stayed up late every night
late till it became early
and I waited
in the midst of the chaos going on inside my
heart
waiting for the world to be quiet again
just so that I could experience what id been
chasing all day
and didn't seem to find it:

peace

so I get on my knees
and I pray

your downfall
was holding on
to your **pride**
and mine was holding on
to my *hope*

sometimes I wonder if years from now
you'll see something that reminds you of me
a song,
a place,
a scent,
a feeling
and I wonder if you'll miss me
and if so
what will you do about it
and the answer is
probably the same you've always done:

n
o
t
h
i
n
g

my feelings woke me up in the middle of the night
and I felt so much
that I felt nothing at all

and at the end
it turned out I was right
unfortunately
you proved me right

but for the first time in years
I didn't want to be

I think I haven't cracked the whole timing thing yet…

I seem to always let go
too early
or
too late

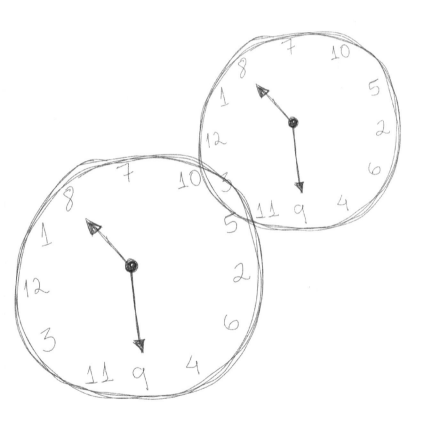

"you know…"
he said as he starred deep into my eyes
"I've always been attracted
to things that make me feel something…
early morning airports,
late night city views,
strong coffee,
this song,
and you
in this moment
right now..."

in your arms
is where I wish I was
instead of in my car
watching the fall leaves
listening to this sad song
and holding on to our memories
as tight as to the hope
that you'll change your mind

but every once in a while
I see something that reminds me of you
and it takes me back in time
back to when you more than just a memory
inside a polaroid picture lost somewhere in my room
back when you gave me a little taste of heaven
and I was living for the hope of it
back when you gave me pain
and I called it love
back when you had me wrapped around your arms
before you slipped away through mine

and there I was again
looking for myself
in the same place I'd lost it

but what am I supposed to do
when the only person
my heart craves comforting
and healing from
is the same one
who broke it

"I'll have the usual"

I say just before I take a sip of my coffee
strong and bitter,
yet I find comfort in it
and with every small sip
hitting me like a bullet train
I feel it rush through my veins
as it wakes me up,
addicting rush,
heavenly bliss,

it never lasts long,
yet I find myself coming back for it everyday,

"I'll have the usual" I say
as I take a sip of your love

for so long
I was so scared
scared to leave
scared to be left
and that fear kept me there
for so long
even when it **hurt**
I stayed
even when I knew I should leave
I stayed
because I was scared
but then I realized
that all along
I had already lost the most important thing:

my freedom

the same way you came into my life
you left it…
suddenly and without a warning

ironic isn't it?
that we were so afraid
to try something new
and risk ruining
what we already had
just to end up here

in the middle of this mess

in a way darker place
than what we deeply feared

If I'm being quite honest
I still don't understand
I really don't
but I'm tired of trying to

so I'm letting you go
not trying to stopping you
you're still free
free to come if you want
but I deserve my freedom too
and it can't be trying to control yours…

next time you walk into an unfamiliar place
and your eyes shift from face to face
looking for mine
till your brain reminds you I'm not there
please remember,
that's what you wanted

next time our song comes on
and nobody around you *gets it*
and you have no one to dance to it with
just remember, that's what you wanted

next time you receive good news
and you pick up your phone
till you realize I'm the only one
you wanna share it with
remember, that's what you wanted

and the next time my heart screams for help
craving your comfort
and I pick up my phone to reach you
i'll remember
that's what you wanted.

I've always thought d i s t a n c e
was my worst enemy
until I understood what it felt like
to miss someone who was right next to you

there was a time
when I thought I'd know you forever
…
but now **look at us**
look at what we became
and look at what we didn't

now I sit here in my room
reading our old texts
listening to our favorite songs
doing anything I can
to feel close to you

when all I want to do
is reach out to you

but I know if even I do
you won't be the one to answer
or at least,
not the one I remember

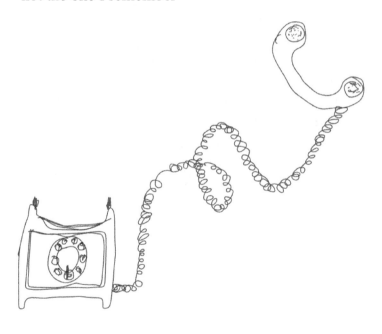

"meek answers"

"what's your favorite color?"
he asked me followed by
a sound of disappointment
when I quickly answered without
hesitation
 "black"
"It sounds like you had a
different answer in mind" I say
"I mean… black isn't a color-"
"its a shade" I interrupt him
he looks away in disappointment
and I do too..

my eyes shift to the little kids
 running around the park
they fill the surroundings with innocent
laughs we've all had
the honor of experiencing
at least once in our lives…

...suddenly my mind brings me to a kitchen
when I am fifty eight years old
drinking my coffee and eating pancakes for
breakfast
when none of this matters anymore

but right now it does

so I turn to him and say
"sometimes when you find something you like
you make an exception for them even though
they might not fit the box people expect them
to"
he didn't answer and I didn't explain
we simply exchanged looks and I know he
understood

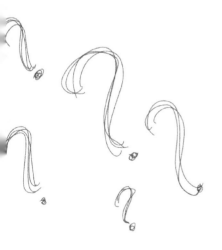

BLAH

      BLAH

            BLAH

I'm so exhausted of this heaviness
I want to write something lighter
something happier

but right now this is what I feel inside
and its so overwhelming
I thought it'd help to

p

   o

      u

        r

           it

into words on this paper

I knew it was over when
your actions had filled every inch in the room
leaving no chairs left on the table
for me to sit all the excuses
I kept making for you

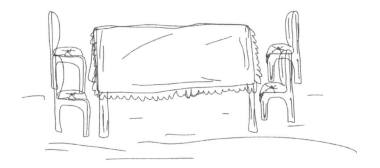

I never knew something could feel
so close to me and so far at the same time...

not a day goes by when I don't think of her
beauty
I stare at her till minutes turn into hours
that turn into a moment where time doesn't
exist

when I'm happy I look at her,
when I'm anxious I look **for** her,

someone once asked me the definition of
elegance
and I showed them a picture of her
her light beautifully paints everything
around her with grace

it doesn't matter who you are
your eyes can't help but to be drawn to her
she is the star of the show
without ever asking for attention.

she goes through changes often
but her essence always remains the same

she is always alone, but never lonely
she keeps my secrets
better than any friend I have ever had

she's never touched me but has comforted me
more than any shoulder I've cried on

she's been there for me more
than any past lover
who's held my hand
and promised to never leave

she can speak to me without ever saying a word

she carefully observes everyone
but not many observe her
and I can't help but to feel pity
for those who miss out on her

I have always loved the sun
it smiles down at us and embraces us with a hug
like a mom wrapping their child in warm
blanket
it keeps life on earth alive and it's graceful rise
in the early mornings reminds us we can always
start over.
but despite all that it provides,
the sun will never understand me
the way **the moon** does…

"oh, what I would do to be his moon."

"I have always loved the sun
it smiles down at us and embraces us with a hug
like a mom wrapping their child in warm
blanket
it keeps life on earth alive and it's graceful rise
in the early mornings reminds us we can always
start over.
but despite all that it provides,
the sun will never understand me the way **the
moon** does…

oh, what I would do to be his moon"

unlike the other guys
in my past
I can't use the excuse
for my peace of mind that
"we didn't get the chance
to become what we wanted to be"
because the truth is
we did
it was right there in front of us
and you walked past it…

I guess there goes the closure
I so desperately needed

your love was like a fire
and I was dancing in between the flames
so focused on the light it brought to my darkness
and the heat that kept my body warm
that I didn't realize…

it was slowly burning me down

I miss the way your eyes reflected the firework
lights on that new years night
I miss the way your voice sounded on the phone
when you called me on the way home from the
airport the first time you heard me cry
I miss the look on your face when our song
came on at that beach restaurant out of town
I miss the way you laughed while watching our
favorite show for the 7th time and eating
chinese takeout at 2am
I miss the excitement all over your face just
before you took the first sip of the coffee when
we stopped at that cute little spot on our first
road trip

and most of all,
I miss the way we loved each other…

…those are the words I would say
those are the memories I would miss
if you hadn't changed your mind
If you hadn't walked away
from this love story
that never happened

"I miss everything we didn't get the chance to become"

"bittersweet"

today I found a wooden box under my bed
it was filled with polaroid pictures
I started shuffling through them
filling their texture on my hands
they carried a fusty smell
that reminded me of my grandma's attic

as I was looking through them
an unexpected feeling of nostalgia overcame me
a surprising mix of bittersweet emotions
soft moments filled with laughs and cries
hellos and goodbyes
sweet moments in time that we'll never get back

so I put the box down and went back out
into the world
with a renewed motive and hope
to create more bittersweet sweet memories

one day
one day i'll gather up the courage
to get up and walk away
but this time I won't look back
and it's in my absence
that you'll realize you already had
what you've been looking for
all along

I'm a hopeless romantic
I'm a sucker for fairy tales
and what a cruel tragedy it was
for you to come into my life
and tear apart
our very own love story

every time
I find myself away from the shore
finally out in the sea
in the midst of waves of hope
every time
I'll catch myself looking out into the horizon
and my eyes will shift from the yellow in the sun
into the blue clear sky that surrounds it
and that deep sad blue
filling every inch of the sky
will remind me of you
and just like that
it starts to rain again…

I could spend days
trying to understand God's love

but how can I make sense
of forgiveness before apologies
of protection without request
of an extended helping hand
without asking for anything in return
of a redeeming, reckless, never ending love

it's sad it **had** to be this way
mainly because
it didn't

I'm tired of writing with so much weight
in my heart
but right now I don't know any other way
maybe
maybe if I put myself in your shoes
on the receiving side of my love
maybe then
I could come up with something
lighter,
sweeter,
happier…

…maybe I could write a poem about **love**
a beautiful,
freeing love
maybe I could write about how it feels to be loved
so deeply you start loving yourself that way
maybe I could write about
how it feels to have someone
know your darkest parts
and still see art when they look at you
maybe I could write about
how safe it feels
when they could leave
but they choose to stay
maybe…
but for now
this is what I can write
with the *love* you're giving me

I used to think
the power was in being "free"
and being able to do whatever your heart desires
but it wasn't till I met Jesus
and surrendered it all
as He took all the weight I'd been carrying
and held me in His arms
that I realized
I was a slave to my own desires
and called it freedom

one day it just hits you
you realize that it's less about
deciding to let them go
and giving them permission to walk away
and more about
accepting that they already have

"time heals"
they would always tell me…
and I believed it for a while
but the truth is
time doesn't heal anything
what it does
is it teaches you how to live with the heartache

you won't find healing until,
you find Jesus

your heart reminds me a lot of a strainer
no matter how much I pour into it
it'll never be *enough* to fill it up

you said you needed space
I can I understand
you said you needed time to think
I can I understand
you said you needed your freedom
I can I understand…
but when you see me with someone else
I hope you can understand.

and I'd ask myself over and over
why I kept going back
haven't I learnt I lesson?

oh I learned my lesson
but every time I looked into your eyes
you made me wanna learn it all over again

"saudade"
is everything we wanted to do
and did it

you have the sweetest soul I've ever *tasted*
but sometimes I wish
I hadn't
because even though it's been a while
and its all far long gone
I still search for you in everyone I meet

"thoughts better off kept inside my mind"

now I sit across from him at the dinner table
eating left over stuffing and mashed potatoes
from thanksgiving
as we try make small talk about how our day
went at work
our eyes are tired and the silence is loud
yet somehow comforting
we glance at the tv while it plays a scene from
The Notebook
"they always make love look so much better in
the movies," he says "it's so unrealistic"
I laugh as I nod my head agreeing as I watch a
scene
where the two young lovers run into the ocean
together…

…I close my eyes as I take another bite and
suddenly Im transported
from that lonely and dark living room
to a place much warmer where I laughed freely
and prayed I'd never leave
I'm taken to all those summer days & nights
we'd spend together making memories that
would haunt me on cold days like these
and just for a second
somewhere in those memories
I find hope that that kind of love is real

119

in the middle of the night
I was woken up
again
by the loud screams
of a familiar sound
I've heard before

oh, my poor aching heart...

before you go and take their advice
please remember that
just because they want the best for you
doesn't mean they know what's best for you

I saw in the look in your eyes
how weak you thought I was
that day I finally cried in front of you
for the first time
but what you didn't know was
it takes a lot more strength
to be vulnerable
than it does to hide it

but that's something you have yet to learn

as exhausted as I was
that night was when I realized
that there's something so special
and peaceful
and peaceful
about being awake at 3am
when the world is still asleep

"I just wanted to understand you"

so I learned to pay close attention to the things
you did
the things you said
and **how** you said them
the way your eyes shifted away when you lied
and how your cheeks flustered when you were
happy
the first song you chose to play when we got in
the car
and the tone in which you picked up the phone
when I called

I was trying to puzzle together
trying to find clues
of what was going on inside your mind
since you didn't have the courage
to tell me yourself

I look at her and I wonder
I wonder why she's still with you
I wonder if she knows
I wonder if she ever looks into your eyes and
sees right through it
I wonder if she sometimes too
wonders

but I really can't blame her for staying
when, for so long,
I did too.

I'm not exactly sure how or when
and mainly why
it happened
but it did
your texts started to get shorter
and taking longer to come through
until they just stopped coming all together

I laid on my bed all night
trying to distract myself
while my heart sank with every hour that went by
and I waited for a message that never came

my music taste
are songs that explain
what my words can't

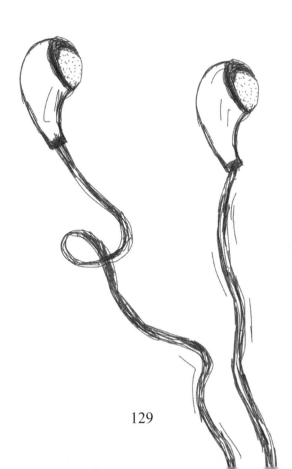

you started out so different
than everyone else I've met before,
just to end up the same way
they all did...

I used to think love was a game
every time I'd play my focus was on how to win
I took notes from my first knock downs
and built an armor around my heart

subconsciously I started training myself
to go into a battlefield
and I'd only head to places where I'd be attacked

I conditioned myself to think like that for so long
that I was caught off guard
when I stepped into your land
and realized
your love was a garden
I didn't need weapons for

and when I unpacked
my bag
and you saw
all that I was
carrying
you grabbed my my
face with tender hands
looked into my eyes
and told me

"we are on the same team"

the truth is
I wasn't perfect
and you weren't either
but what we had
it felt so close to it…

"well, you live and you learn"
I tell them with a forced laugh

but deep down inside I know
I never intended for us to become a lesson
but a story we'd tell our kids someday

I could spend hours
trying to explain
trying to put it into words
how much I love you

but if you just took a moment
and looked into my eyes
they would tell you everything my words can't

"why are you so scared?"
you asked me with confusion in your eyes
"because I've been so wrong in the past…
and my heart cant afford to be wrong again…"

I used to love riding my pink bike
it used to make me feel so free

until one day I was writing down a hill
the wind was blowing on my hair
I was having too much fun I forgot to look
where I was heading
and I got too comfortable, perhaps too excited
and I fell
I fell really hard

and it hurt.

after that, I was scared to ever ride a bike again

-this poem is not about bikes.

now I understand why they say to be careful
who you make memories with
because those things
they can last a lifetime…

we are both so different now
life's shaped us
I mean look at us
you've changed so much
I barely recognize you
but if I look closely
there's one thing that remains the same
there's one thing I remember
your eyes
because it's the same ones I looked at when I
got to experience some of the most beautiful
moments in my life

don't you dare ask me
why I look this way
when you're the reason
why I'm not okay

you lacked self love
and didn't have the courage
to go for what was best for you
(me)

while I…
well I did the same
I lacked self love
and didn't have the courage
to go for what was best for me
(someone else)

it turns out
we were more alike than I thought

and one day
I couldn't stand it anymore
and all I wanted was to ask you
how you felt about me
how you **really** felt
and right before I did
I decided to take my own advice
and wait
wait to see if you'd come to me
and by the time I went to sleep that night
I had my answer

what does falling in love feel like?
I was asked by a friend today
and I answered

"love feels like laughing with your best friend at
3am when you're trying to be quiet cause her
parents are asleep
love feels like strawberry ice cream with
sprinkles on summer days as a child
love feels like a labyrinth where you find
loyalty at every corner no matter which turn you
take
it feels like diving in the ocean for the first time

but love can also feel like a bee sting sometimes
unexpected and unpredictable
and debatably unavoidable
one thing I know for sure about what love feels
like
is that you must experience it for yourself in
order to understand
no words, songs, poems, can do it justice"

looking back at it now
I can see it clear as day
and I'd never thought I'd say this but
I have never been more thankful
for something not working out in my life
the way I wanted it to

and when I asked you how you felt
deep down inside
I didn't expect you to tell me the truth
only because I knew
you were also lying to yourself

pine trees and snowy mountains surrounds me
hot chocolate in my hands and a warm blanket
on my lap
my favorite childhood movie plays on the tv
and I play with you hair as you smile up at me
I look up and thank God
for how good He is

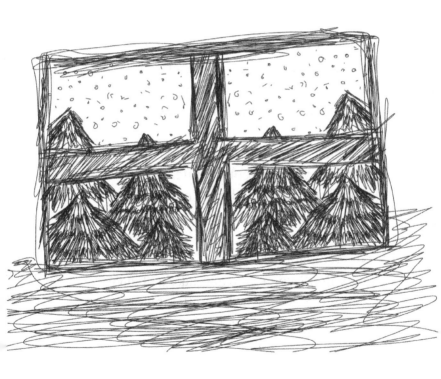

dim lights
full room
no fights
the clock marks noon

all eyes on me
the music flows
look and you'll see
how my eyes glow

long dresses flowing
we mold this dance like it's clay
love for one another is growing
while we connect in a new way

who knew dance could do this
who knew music could unite
but if you had asked me I'd never miss
the truth I've known my whole life

so go on and break out of your comfort
why don't you come and take a chance
cause the time won't stop ticking
so come join us for a dance

you pushed my love away
you refused to accept it

but I think it's because
you thought the love I had to offer
is somewhat similar
to the one you've offered me

tell me
it's terrifying, isn't it?

close your eyes
and think about a beautiful human in your mind…

now explain what makes it **beautiful**

and what makes it **human**

and there were always these moments,
where I'd just stand there in awe,
looking around me,
at the view,
the people,
the opportunities,
all the life laying ahead of me,
and the world would slow down for a minute,
my heart would fill up with peace and hope,
and it was moments like those,
as simple as they were,
that wouldn't trade for anything in this world.

let's go on a roadtrip
pack up your bags and get in the car
we'll stop for food on the way
and find a place to stay
I want to explore this world with you
I want to see new sunsets
meet new faces
try new foods
so lets not waste time
lets make some memories
to tell our kids someday

I want a love
that makes me feel
the way music does…

I wanted it to be you so bad
and I would've done anything
for you
for us

and the sad part is
I did
but it still wasn't enough to keep you

you exchanged something real
for temporary pleasure
at the expense
of my heart

tell me,
was it worth it?

and I watched you laugh in the passenger seat
singing your favorite song at the top of your lungs
giving life to each word that came out of your lips
letting go of all your worries
as the summer breeze blew through your hair
you were looking at me with wild eyes
full of love
the sun was kissing your skin
you held your hand out the window
and your heart out on your sleeve
and it was at that moment that I knew

I never knew what version of you I was going to get
and the unpredictability
that hope
kept me coming back each time

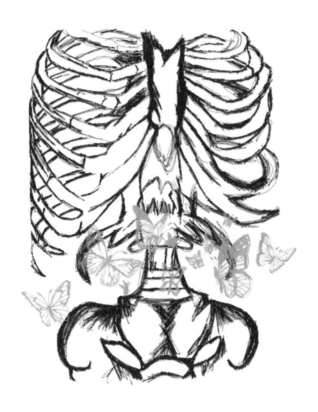

I hate that I feel like you put me in a situation
where I have to pick between
losing you

                                              or myself

the problem is
I never learned how to just like things
or people…
I always let it consume me

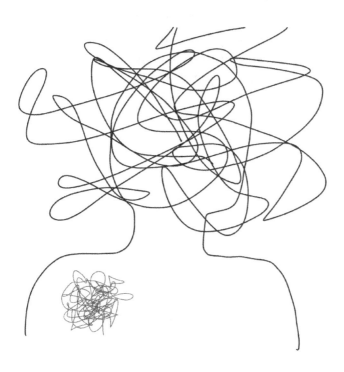

"do you regret it"

"loving you?"

"yes…"

"…"

"if you could go back in time would you do it again?"

"in a heartbeat"

"even knowing it'd turn out this way?"

"I'd rather get my heart broken by you a thousand times than live a life without knowing your love…"

I wish I could climb inside your mind
and dive into your thoughts
and maybe then
I could try to make sense of it all

"endless cycle"

I make my bed every morning,
and somehow,
it always ends up messy at the end of the day.

I wash my clothes every week,
and yet,
its always dirty when I want to wear it.

I check off to-do lists every day,
and still,
there's always more to get done.

I pour my heart out to you every day,
and yet,
I still feel like I need to earn it when I need it most.

I'm tired of this endless cycle...

it wasn't until one sunny afternoon,
when someone else came into my garden
and picked up my flowers
making a garment out of it
that I learned
the problem wasn't my seeds
but the soil I was placing them in

"the first step of moving on"

I thought moving on would be fun
I thought it'd be like the songs
the ones you sing in the car with your friends on
a friday night
I thought it'd taste like *freedom*

so I started talking to strangers
releasing the idea of us
little by little
the one which I held on to tightly
for so long

but it wasn't until
his lips were on mine
and my mind remained on you
and all I could taste was **bitterness**
that I learned:

the first step of moving on wasn't distraction
it was **healing**

and it's eye opening to think
that this whole time you've been pushing me away
I've been blaming you
for doing the exact same thing
I've been doing all along

searching the world
for a love
that was already in front of you...

maybe one day
years from now
I'll call you and ask you to talk
and we'll meet up
and we'll grab a coffee
and we'll sit somewhere nice and have a long
conversation
and we'll talk about what we were
and what we weren't
we'll talk about the things we said
and the things we didn't say
and we'll remember old memories
and we'll laugh at ourselves
and maybe tear up a little

maybe one day…

I used to blame myself
think I wasn't good enough
I'd cry over and over again
then turn around
and convince myself you were the one with holes

and then I'd drain myself
trying to fill you up
leaving us both empty

if I only I would've known…
we will never be able to find peace
within each other
if we haven't first found it
in Jesus

but if only I had known
how loved I was

I wouldn't have been out there day and night
begging
so desperately
for a love that's already been given to me

this is not the type of person I am
that is not the type of "love" I want

but,

I can't blame you for misunderstanding who I was
when I did too...

"but where were you
when I needed you
when I cried out for help
you said
you promised
you'd always look out for me
and when I was down at my lowest
so helpless
I screamed for you
till I lost my voice
and I waited
but you never came
how could you leave me like that?
I was in so much pain

I thought I needed you
but I didn't know
you were the one
i needed to be protected from"

"an honest letter from me to old myself"

God taught me
how to love
by loving me first

and He taught me how to forgive
by forgiving me first

I never knew pain could feel numb
I never knew love could feel so out of reach

until I had poured all of my heart on the table
in front of you
and I heard your stomach growl
as I watched you take a good look at it
and walk away

there was just something about seeing you
reject what I was offering you
when we both knew you were hungry for it

I was hunted by the fears of my past
screaming at me that it'd never work out
but something kept *whispering* to me
to not lose hope

and today
I am so glad I didn't

I looked at you with confusion
after I made you run out of patience
and you chose to stay

I didn't understand
I thought it wasn't normal
because for so long
my version of normal
wasn't.

there's so much beauty all around us
life and love flow abundantly from within
if only we stopped chasing it in the world
and took a moment to realize that
we already have all we could ever need:

God.

its been so long since I have seen **you**
or at least this version of you
with a light smile on your face
and that childhood innocence in your eyes

your joy is evident
through the lightness in your voice
when you talk about life
and the way you carry yourself

I wasn't sure I was ever going to
see you like this again
and I am so glad you didn't lose hope
I'm so glad you didn't give up

"a conversation with the one in the mirror"

you gave me a love I didn't know I needed
a love I couldn't even have asked for
because I didn't know it existed

until I met you

"white canvas"

it was 3:49pm on a cold November day
when my little sister walked up to me
she had a canvas in her hands and a smile on
her face
jumping of excitement as she showed me her
artwork
what once was a white canvas
was now filled with gold sparkles and
butterflies stickers everywhere
so chaotic yet beautiful
I smiled at the thought that she had taken all the
things she loved
and just glued it all together on there
trying to make the best of it

I told her I loved it
that it was full of full of trials and errors
but the beauty was that it was unique

I told her that not everyone
was going to understand it
some might even judge it
but as grandma always told us "the beauty is in
the eye of the beholder" …

…and I laughed at the irony of it all
as I thought about it on the way home
when I realized
her and I had a lot more in common than I
imagined
only that her canvas represented my life…

"I want a simple life"

not "settling" simple
not "basic" simple
not "boring" or "repetitive" simple
I want a simple where I find the beauty in
everything surrounding me
a simple where I find pleasure in seeking to
serve rather than to be served
a simple where I create the fun instead of
relying on my circumstances
a simple where I'm not afraid to ask my Father
for things I need because I have learned a while
ago that He loves His children
a simple where my heart is in a constant state of
thankfulness to my God
a simple where I don't follow the world's rules
and depend on people, money, fame, or the
weather to start **living**

despite it all,
I still hope the best for you.

I didn't understand loneliness
until you were right there with me
but your heart was far away

but it wasn't till I found myself
embraced by surrender
and with arms wide open
to the new and unknown
stepping out in faith
that I understood

you can still feel safe in the fall
when you know Who's going to catch you

be wise with you choices
love is something way too important in life
for your to compromise on

I normally like sitting under this tree
finding comfort in the shadows
and relief from the the loudness of the world
but today it seems no matter where I go
I can't seem to flee this feeling of being blue
without you

the loudness I so desperately want to escape
comes from within
I look at old pictures in attempt to ease the pain
trying to feel close to you again
in the midst of this mess
I find hope I can still find comfort elsewhere

maybe I'll go visit my hometown
and stop by at my grandma's house
drink coffee with her while she braids my hair
and tells me to focus on God
cause life isn't always fair

maybe there I can practice my gentleness
so that from my lips
soft words will come out next time we speak

"I'm sorry and please come back"

there are days
when I just sit there quietly
and I watch you talk
observing
letting my eyes wander as you speak
reading every line in between your words
studying every inch of your features
till my eyes grow sore
and they do
but they never get tired
of looking at you

the way you make me feel
is a feeling I believe
everyone in this world should get to experience
at least once in a lifetime

maturing is when you realize
you have to stop walking around
with your arms open
only expecting people to pour out
good things to you
and bring you happiness
and you start taking responsibility
to ignite it yourself

this moment with you is precious
I wish I could bottle it up
and just carry it with me
everywhere I go
in case I am missing you a little extra
and wanna go back to it

what you failed to understand is that
I didn't necessarily
need you to be there for me all the time
I just needed to know that you would if needed it

growing up is
learning that just because they were your first love
it doesn't mean they were your best love
they gave you a glimpse of what's out there
waiting for you

there is so much love to feel
so much life to experience
and you better get to it

you don't know…
you don't know but I tried
I took every little strength I had left in my body
and tried to crawl out of there
but I couldn't
and when I finally reached my hand up for help
God held it
and it's through Him that I'm here today
and it's through Him that I'm able to look you
in the eyes today
and choose love instead of hate
because
He first loved me

and one day I realized
it was never about possession
and indeed about appreciation

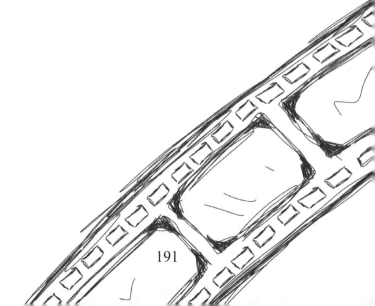

I knew you existed
Ive been looking for you
my whole life
In every love song
I've sang to you
In every sunset I've watched
wondering where you were
In every memory I've lived
wishing you were there
In every person I met
looking for you in them
holding tight to every hope I ever had to ever find
love

they say you can't miss something you never had
so for a long time I wondered,
how is it that I missed you
before I ever met you

one day you're going to meet someone
and you'll fall in love with them
and I mean it when I say
with everything in me
I hope you never have to go through what I did
I hope they don't do to you
what you did to me
but if for some reason
you find yourself
in the middle of tears
drowning in an ocean of pain
holding on for dear life
to the pieces left of your heart
I hope that with your heartbreak
you decide to make something beautiful out of it
just like I am
right now
through this book

the end.

note to reader:

I'm sorry…
I'm sorry things didn't go as you planned. I'm sorry you're not even disappointed at this point because you already expected it to turn out that way. I'm sorry you've been hurt by people who didn't know you well enough to know your heart and, I'm even more sorry you got hurt by the ones who did. I'm sorry about the words that have been said to you, the words that pierced through your heart and weighed so heavily on you that you repeated it to yourself over and over till you stared believing it.
I'm sorry that the person who was supposed to show how loved you were didn't have it in them to do so. I'm sorry you put your hopes on the wrong things and people or maybe they weren't necessarily the wrong people but just people, and people make mistakes. I'm sorry you sold yourself short because you felt as though you weren't deserving of good things, because maybe that's what you've been told before… I'm sorry that a future where you're truly, truly happy may seem like a made up fairytale and I'm sorry that "it's going to be okay" may seem like easy and empty words people say to make others feel better when they have no idea what to do either…

the truth is: I may not be able to help much with these words on the paper right now but I do know Who can.

what I wanna tell you is that there is hope. there is life ahead, and not just life as you know it: little moments of joy here and there. there is a full and joyful life ahead, there is so, so much love for you, you just need to reach out and embrace it. the grace, the hope, purpose and the love you've searched around the world and failed time and time again to find - only to see yourself more lost than before. I wanna tell you that it exists and it's within your reach right at this moment. Love came down to earth and walked around us. He died for us so that we don't have to suffer the misery of living in our sins forever and -contrary to what the enemy may have you believed your whole life: you can start over, you can begin again, you can be born again. just reach back to God's hand and accept His love.

with **Jesus** it WILL get better.
because of Him you are **forgiven**.
and through Him you are made **new**.

I hope you know how loved you are -and if you don't yet, I hope you have the courage to step closer to Jesus and allow Him to show you.

about the author:

Meet Carol, a 24-year-old Brazilian poet who loves to write and paint with words. Her poetry is all about connecting with people and helping them understand their feelings. She believes in the power of art to express emotions and make others feel understood. Carol's first book is like a diary of her heart over the years—a collection of thoughts and experiences about love, heartbreak, and growth. In her poems, Carol invites readers to feel with her, to see themselves in her words. Her writing celebrates vulnerability and reminds us that everyone's journey is filled with both joy and pain. Through her heartfelt verses, she hopes to bring comfort and inspiration to those who read her book, encouraging them to embrace their own stories with courage and compassion and never give up on love.
Connect with her: @itscarolchaves

Made in the USA
Monee, IL
17 December 2024